Scholastic Publications Ltd.,
10 Earlham Street, London WC2H 9RX, UK

Scholastic Inc.,
730 Broadway, New York, NY 10003, USA

Scholastic Tab Publications Ltd.,
123 Newkirk Road, Richmond Hill,
Ontario L4C 3G5, Canada

Ashton Scholastic Pty. Ltd.,
P O Box 579, Gosford, New South Wales,
Australia

Ashton Scholastic Ltd.,
165 Marua Road, Panmure, Auckland 6,
New Zealand

First published by Scholastic Publications Limited, 1988
Text copyright © John Cunliffe, 1988
Illustrations copyright © Scholastic Publications Limited and
Woodland Animations Limited, 1988

ISBN 0 590 70998 4

Made and printed in Hong Kong
Typeset in Times Roman by AKM Associates (UK) Ltd,
Ajmal House, Hayes Road, Southall, London

Postman Pat
Gets a Pet

Story by **John Cunliffe** *Pictures by* **Joan Hickson**
From the original Television designs by **Ivor Wood**

Hippo Books
in association with André Deutsch

Every day, Postman Pat sets out with his good cat Jess by his side. But there was a time, a long time ago, when Pat had no cat. He was alone in his red van, and he had no Jess to talk to as he drove along.

It all begin with the white mice. Every Saturday, Pat, and Sara, and Julian, go to Pencaster market in the Greendale bus, to do their shopping. One Saturday was busier than ever. There was such a lot of shopping to do. Pat and Sara filled their bags and baskets with potatoes, and onions, and oranges, and sprouts, and lettuces, and cheese.

"Could you hold the carrots, Julian?" said Sara.

"Could you hold the apples and grapefruit, Julian?" said Pat.

Julian's arms were full of shopping, and he thought it would never end. He was so tired. There was a long queue at the butcher's, and another at the fish shop. Sara and Pat looked in every shop, and stopped to talk to all their friends.

"Oh, come on!" said Julian.

"Be patient," said Sara.

They walked past the toy-shop, full of trains, and planes, and dolls. They walked past a shop full of radios and cassette players. They did not stop. Then they did stop, to talk to Miss Hubbard.

"Look!" said Julian.

They had stopped outside the pet-shop. There, in the window, was a cage full of white mice. One of the mice was looking out at Julian, and twitching its whiskers.

"A little white mouse," said Julian. "I'd love a little white mouse."

"Ooooh," said Pat, "I'm not sure I like mice."

"I always wanted one when I was little," said Sara, "but my mum would never let me."

"I'd love a mouse," said Julian.

"You'd need two or three, to keep each other company," said Sara. "Well, we could go in and look at them."

Sara and Julian went in the pet-shop. Pat stayed outside, talking to Miss Hubbard, or, at least, listening to her. He was saying "Goodbye!" to Miss Hubbard, just as Julian and Sara came out again, carrying a cage with four mice in it.

"What have you got there?" said Pat.

"Mini-tigers," said Sara.

"Aren't they lovely?" said Julian.

"Mmmmmm. . . ." said Pat. "I'm not too sure . . . Ouch!"

He had poked his finger between the bars of the cage, and a little brown mouse gave it a good nip.

"You frightened it," said Sara. "That's why it bit you. They have to get used to you."

"I don't think I'll get used to it," said Pat.

"What shall we call them?" said Julian.

"You can call that one Nipper," said Pat.

"And the white ones are Bess and Bill," said Julian.

"And the black-and-white one's Jess," said Sara.

It was soon time to catch the bus home to Greendale. Many of their friends were on the bus, with their bags of shopping. They saw Miss Hubbard, and Granny Dryden, and all the Thompsons. The Reverend Timms jumped in, just as the bus was getting ready to start.

"Can't be bothered with the old car on Saturdays," he said. "There's just nowhere to park. Hello, what have you got there? White mice? Bless me, I had some when I was a boy. What a lovely present."

All went well until Julian put the cage of mice on the seat beside him, and looked out of the window to wave at Peter Fogg on his tractor. When he looked back at the mice, there was Nipper, sitting on top of the cage, looking all about him with great interest. He had never seen a bus before, and meant to find out all about it.

"Dad," said Julian. "Quick! One's got out."

Pat stretched his hand out. Sara pulled it back.

"You don't want another bite," she said. "I'll get my gloves on, then I can pick it up."

But before she could do anything, Nipper jumped off the cage, ran along the seat, up the back and over, and jumped into Dorothy Thompson's lap.

She screamed,
  "A mouse! A mouse! Help!"

And she jumped up, shaking Nipper off
her coat and on to the floor. Now it ran
between the Reverend's legs. He tried to
catch it, but it was too quick for him. It
was away along the length of the bus,
making people jump and squeal as it
tickled their feet.

The driver stopped the bus in a lay-by, to see what the trouble was, and joined in the hunt for the mouse. Everyone tried to catch that little mouse. And whilst they were busy, the other three squeezed out between the bars of the cage, and ran for freedom.

What a rumption there was in the Greendale bus that day! Some people were creeping about on their hands and knees, looking for the mice and shouting to each other, whilst others sat with their feet tucked up on the seats out of the way of mouse-nips.

It was the Reverend Timms who put things to rights, in the end. He said, in his best church voice, "Dear friends. If you will all sit still and quiet I'll catch those mice in a trice. I kept mice as a boy, and I know what to do."

At the sound of his voice, everyone calmed down and sat quietly. The Reverend borrowed a plastic bucket that Granny Dryden had bought in the market, and some crumbs of cake from Miss Hubbard. He put the cake in the bucket and the bucket on the floor, sideways, and waited. Everyone sat still. You would have thought there was no one in that bus, it was so quiet. But you could hear a scurrying and a scratching, as the four mice explored the bus. And then a patter-patter sound, when they found the bucket, and their little paws tapped on the smooth plastic. Then a tiny munching sound, as they ate the cake.

The Reverend picked up the bucket, and held it the right way up. There were the four little mice, in the bottom of the bucket, and no matter what they did, they could not get out again. The plastic was too slippery for them to climb.

Granny Dryden said they could borrow her bucket, if they gave it a good washing out afterwards.

"It's no good you putting them back in that cage," she said. "They'll only get out again."

So the mice had to live in the bucket for a day or two, until Pat could think what to do.

When Mrs Goggins heard about the trouble with the mice, she said,

"If you get a bigger pet it won't squeeze between the bars. Why don't you get a hamster? They're lovely. There were some folks on holiday last summer; they had one, and it was a real beauty. They used to bring it in to show me. It never bit anyone, and the little girl loved it."

So Pat asked Julian, and he said, "All right," and Pat caught the bus to Pencaster on Tuesday afternoon, with the cage and the bucket of mice, and came back with a hamster in the cage and the empty bucket.

The hamster didn't bite, and Julian was quite fond of it. All went well until the day he said, "The poor thing must get tired of being in that cage all the time, and running round and round in that wheel. Do you think we could let it out for a run round the carpet?"

It seemed such a quiet creature, and so sweet-tempered, that Sara said,

"Well, I'm sure it wouldn't do any harm to let it out for a little while, if you keep your eye on it. It's too big to go down a mousehole."

But the hamster went behind the settee, and wouldn't come out. And when Sara and Julian moved the settee away from the wall, there was no sign of the hamster. And when Pat came home, there was no tea ready, and Sara and Julian were creeping about all over the house looking for the hamster, and calling to it, but there was neither sight nor sound of it. Then Pat said, "What's this hole under the settee?"

And Sara said, "What hole?. . . .Oh!"

And they saw the tooth marks all round the hole, and knew who had made it. Then Pat took the back off the settee to see if the hamster was inside. There was a pile of sawdust, where the hamster had been nibbling, but no hamster. Then Julian looked behind the television set, and saw a hole in the skirting board, and Pat moved the television, so that they could see it properly. When Alf called in to borrow a bag of sugar, they showed him the hole.

"That's a hamster-hole, all right," he said. "They love gnawing wood. It's in their nature. It'll be right under the floor, now, nibbling away to its heart's content. You'll have to have the floor up. You'll never get it out. It'll have the floor caving in, after a time."

"Oh, dear," said Sara, "that'll never do. It'll cost a fortune."

"You ought to get a dog," said Alf. "They make the best pet you can have. And they're useful for getting sheep in."

"We haven't got any sheep," said Pat.

"No, but you've got a hamster," said Alf. "Perhaps our Towser could get it out."

He brought his little dog in. It snuffled at the hole, and wagged its tail like mad, but it couldn't get the hamster out.

But Pat had an idea.

"I'll catch the hamster," he said.

"You'll never get it in a bucket," said Alf.

"No, but I bet you I can get it," said Pat.

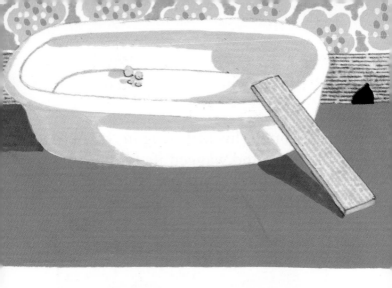

That night, after Julian had gone to bed, Pat got his old baby-bath out, and put it near to the hole the hamster had made. He put some hamster food in the empty bath. Then he found a long piece of wood and leaned it against the bath. The wood made a path up to the edge of the bath. The sides of the bath were high and slippery.

"Are you thinking of giving that hamster a bath?" said Sara.

"It might need one," said Pat. "But it must be getting hungry. When we've gone to bed, it's sure to come out.

The idea is, that it will walk up the wood, jump in the bath for the food, and not be able to climb out again up the slippery sides."

"It's not as daft as that," said Sara. "It'll never work. Hamsters have more brains than mice."

When Pat went to bed, he lay awake in the dark. When all the house was quiet, there was, Pat felt sure, a tiny sound of little paws and nibbling teeth. Pat crept downstairs, with his torch. There, in the empty bath, sat a rather dusty hamster, blinking in the light!

On Wednesday afternoon, Pat took the
hamster back to Pencaster in its cage, and
came back with a large sheep-dog.

Julian called the dog Bess, after one of the mice. He loved her. She was a very lively dog, and had to go for a long walk every day. She never sat still. When Pat was out with his letters, and Julian was at school, Sara and Bess walked the hills all over Greendale.

Then Sara got a job, in the council office in Pencaster. What would happen to Bess?

"She'll have to come with me, in my van," said Pat.

But, oh dear, Bess was hopeless in Pat's van. She wouldn't stay in her basket. One day she chewed the corner of a parcel.

She jumped out and chased hens. She ran
off looking for sheep to round up, and it
took Pat an hour to find her. She even
followed Pat and growled at Miss
Hubbard when she came out for a parcel.

"Well," said Miss Hubbard, "I've heard of postmen being chased by dogs, but never t'other way round," as Pat shooed Bess back to the van. "That dog needs training, Pat."

"You're right," said Pat, "and I've no notion about how to do it."

"Colonel Forbes is on the look out for another sheep-dog," said Miss Hubbard. "And he's a dab at training dogs. He'd soon get her into shape. Why don't you have a word with him?"

"I will," said Pat.

Colonel Forbes was delighted.

"She's just the dog for me," he said. "Bring her round on Monday, and we'll make a start with her."

So it was all settled. But Pat, and Sara, and Julian were sad. They would miss Bess, far more than they had missed the hamster and the mice. As Pat said, "For all her faults, she's a loving creature. But . . . I can't be having the post late, whilst I'm chasing all over Greendale to find her when she takes it into her head to wander off. Silly lass!"

Monday came. Julian looked tearful as he said "Goodbye" to Bess.

"Don't take on," said Pat. "You'll be able to go round to the Colonel's to see her, any time you like."

"I know," said Julian, but he still looked tearful.

Pat had delivered all his letters, and it was time to take Bess to Colonel Forbes. Pat drove along, with Bess by his side. He felt tearful himself. Just as they were passing Alf Thompson's bottom meadow, Bess began to make a fuss.

"Oh, you don't want to get out, do you?" said Pat. "Just when we're a bit late."

But Bess did want to get out. She barked and whined until Pat stopped the van.

"Be quick, then," said Pat.

Bess jumped out. But she still whined at Pat.

"What is it now?" said Pat in a cross voice.

41

She wanted him to get out and look.
Pat came. Bess led him to a cardboard
box, stuck in the hedge. She sniffed and
whined and wagged her tail. She nosed at
the box.

"What is it, Bess?" said Pat.

Pat lifted the lid of the box.

"Well, I'll be blessed!" said Pat. "How
did you know that was there?"

Curled up in the bottom of the box was
a little black-and-white kitten. Pat picked
it up gently, and it opened its eyes and
mewed at him.

"Poor little thing," said Pat. "Who can
have left you there?"

Bess gave it a kiss with her long wet
tongue that made it sneeze.

"Good girl," said Pat.

And this is how Pat arrived home that day, without Bess, but with a kitten tucked up in his warm coat.

"Let's call it Jess," said Julian.

And they did. They all loved Jess. He didn't run away, or chase hens, or chew holes in the floor, or make people scream in the bus. He has ridden in the van every day with Pat, from that day to this. Pat says,

"He's grand company, is our Jess."

As for Bess, she became a very good sheep-dog. She loves nothing better than a good day out working the sheep on the fells; and the shepherd often brings her to see Pat, and Sara, and Julian, and her old friend Jess.